I0543561

Amazigh
Folk Tales

Amazigh
Folk Tales

Edited by Tahir Shah

The Scheherazade Foundation

The Scheherazade Foundation CIC
85 Great Portland Street
London
W1W 7LT
United Kingdom

www.SF.Charity
info@SF.Charity

First published by The Scheherazade Foundation CIC, 2025

AMAZIGH FOLK TALES

© THE SCHEHERAZADE FOUNDATION

Tahir Shah asserts the right to be identified as the Author of the Work
in accordance with the Copyright, Designs and Patents Act 1988.
A CIP catalogue record for this title is available from the British Library.

ISBN 978-1-915311-65-8

CONTENTS

Introduction	1
Tislit & the Seven Trials	9
Tarek & the Spell of Flight	15
The Eye of the Future	23
The Golden Hen	29
Tahar & the Little Sparrow	35
Yassin, the Serpent, & the Magician's Box	41
The Tale of Tasnin & Amar	47
The Tale of Ayyad & the Hidden Treasure	53
The Tree of Dying Stars	59
The Weaver & the Endless Thread	65
The Mountain of Forgiveness	71
The Singing Well	77
The Tale of Aksel & the Lion	83
The Wisdom of the Elderly Weaver	89
The Tale of Yamina & the Star of the Desert	95
The Tale of the Generous Shepherd	101
The Journey to the Singing Tree	107
The Tale of the Mechanical Horse	113
The Lesson of the Stone	119
The Magical Tarboush	125
The Tale of the Treasure Map	131
The Tale of the Magic Coin	137
The Mirror of Aksil	143

The Flying Carpet   149

The Tale of the Sword of Tamellalt   155

The Dog & the Cat   161

The Tale of the Moon's Lesson   167

Introduction

Twenty years ago, I moved from London with my wife and young family, to an ancient, rambling mansion on the edge of Casablanca.

Back then, Dar Khalifa, 'The Caliph's House', was located squarely in the middle of a sprawling shantytown. Almost everyone living there was Amazigh (formerly referred to as 'Berber').

From the first weeks and months of my new Moroccan life, I grasped that in the kingdom nothing was as it seemed. Although never explained to me, or even openly discussed, I gradually came to understand more of the Amazigh community and culture, and the value system which lies at its heart. Unlike the ostentation of some Arab society, the Amazigh ways are all about understatement, and never dreaming of sticking out.

Beyond all else, it's a society founded on a bedrock of utter moral rectitude.

I will give you an example of something that happened to me last week.

There's a gaping leak in Dar Khalifa's roof, so I went to a local hardware store, known in Morocco as a *droguerie*. The shop I visited was up the hill, and is one of hundreds of tiny emporiums – which sell everything from plungers to plastic sheeting.

1

Every single one of them is Amazigh-owned.

Smaller than most, the particular *droguerie* I went to, for a handful of roof-nails, is owned by four brothers. Rather like Russian dolls that fit neatly into one another, the brothers all look the same, but each is slightly larger and older than the last.

Two decades ago, I used to go to the *droguerie* all the time. Over a year or two, I spent a fortune there, buying anything and everything needed for the restoration of Dar Khalifa.

The other day, when I dropped by, each of the four brothers gasped.

They began chattering excitedly in tashelhit to one another.

I exclaimed how happy I was to see them all again.

Each of the brothers returned the sentiment, thanking God for my arrival. I assumed their high spirits was because I had previously been a good customer, and was likely to be one again.

Just before I placed my order for roof-nails, the oldest of the brothers stepped forwards, his expression solemn.

'We have waited for this day for a long time,' he said.

'For a long, long time,' the other three brothers intoned.

'I'm going to place a big order of roof-nails,' I announced joyously.

The brothers sighed in time with one another.

'We are not asking for more business,' the second brother declared. 'You see, the last time you came here, we overcharged you by five dirhams – for which we apologize sincerely.'

The third brother stepped forwards.

And, taking a coin from a shelf above the counter, he handed it to me, his head dipped in a bow.

All four brothers rejoiced.

'Thank God!' they exclaimed. 'At last, our debt has been repaid!'

What I've just told you of the brothers at the *droguerie* up the hill could be a folktale from the Amazigh community from which they come. That's because the culture is based completely on a set of values that quite easily puts the rest of us to shame.

At the best of times, folktales are complex vessels of cultural wisdom, and are far more than mere entertainments. In many ways, they're the guiding force of a community, a lifeblood, passed down through generations like a baton.

But Amazigh folklore is quite exceptional in the way it acts as a moral compass for wider society. In the collection of folktales presented here, the repetition, the core values, and the profound interconnectedness of tales, come together to illuminate the extraordinarily high moral standing of Amazigh heritage.

Repetition is a hallmark of oral storytelling, and these folktales exemplify its effectiveness. My own personal study of Amazigh stories, made over the decades I have lived in Morocco, I have been fascinated at the way so many tales incorporate the same dynamic arc, and even the same types of trials and tribulations, and ultimate resolution.

Within individual stories, repeated phrases and motifs lend rhythm and memorability, making it easier for both the listener and the teller to be sucked in, and to benefit from the many layers. Consider for instance the trials faced by 'Tislit

& the Seven Trials' – each challenge echoes the one before, reinforcing the tale's central message of resilience.

Across the collection, familiar structures recur – quests, moral tests, and moments of spellbinding transformation. Such patterns evoke a sense of continuity and shared human experience, offering listeners a framework within which to interpret fresh challenges. By weaving repetition into the stories, ancient Amazigh culture has ensured that these narratives resonate while adapting to changing times.

Values, such as duty, respect, honour, and community, form a moral bedrock on which the tales are framed. In 'Tahar & the Little Sparrow', for instance, the lesson revolves around respect for all beings, whether human or animal. Similarly, 'The Mountain of Forgiveness' teaches the transformative power of humility and atonement. Storytellers act as custodians of cultural values, using the folktale as a 'container' to preserve and transmit the ethical framework of their society – moral education, imparted with warmth and subtlety.

One of the most remarkable aspects of Amazigh folktales is their similarity to stories from other parts of the world. The story of 'The Golden Hen' echoes European fairy tales like 'Jack and the Beanstalk', with its themes of humble beginnings and magical riches. Meanwhile, 'The Tale of Yamina & the Star of the Desert' shares common motifs with Arabian and African tales, considering journeys of selflessness and perseverance.

This interconnectedness reflects cultural exchanges that have long flourished along trade and pilgrimage routes, for which Morocco has been a key crossroads since antiquity.

The Amazigh, as a people with roots across North Africa, and stretching down deep into the continent's hinterland, have drawn upon and contributed to a shared human repository of folklore.

Until recently, Amazigh traditions relied almost exclusively on oral tradition to preserve their stories. This reliance, imbued the act of storytelling with a sacred quality, as tales were not merely recited but performed, alive with gestures, tone, and audience interaction. Storytelling sessions were communal events, fostering bonds between generations.

Each retelling was an act of cultural preservation and reinvention, ensuring stories remained relevant to contemporary listeners. Even as the Amazigh world modernizes, this oral legacy serves as a powerful reminder of both the vitality and adaptability of the culture.

As elsewhere, in Amazigh culture, it's often the women who have been the custodians of these tales, passing them down to children in the home.

The tales, told in a mother's or grandmother's voice, carry strict moral lessons. The role of women as storytellers has been pivotal in shaping the cultural identity of the Amazigh people.

Through their storytelling, women imparted not only entertainment but also a sense of both belonging and continuity. In their hands, the folktale became a tool of empowerment, bridging the past and the future, ensuring that the values and wisdom of their ancestors would endure.

During their childhood at Dar Khalifa, my children – Ariane and Timur – were raised by Zeinab, the kindest and wisest housekeeper on earth. Zeinab lived in a shack in the shantytown, a stone's throw from us, and used to recite Amazigh stories to the children – from the moment she arrived in the morning, until the moment she left at night.

In the long afternoons, she used to feed Ariane and Timur lunch in the kitchen, a spoon in either hand – open mouths being plied with food.

As she fed them, she would recount a tale, one she herself had heard and reheard in her own childhood.

When the children stopped eating, Zeinab stopped with the story.

One afternoon, I blustered into the kitchen, part of a manuscript for a book I was writing about Moroccan stories in my hand.

An epic of hope, redemption, truth, and lost love was being played out.

Pausing, I took in Ariane and Timur mouths wide open, ears sharply tuned, with Zeinab mid-performance.

Out of all the overwhelming moments I experienced in those early years – or, indeed, witnessed since, it was the most profound.

Right there at the kitchen table, a chain of transmission was taking place.

A chain of transmission began centuries ago, it was like a magical alchemy drawn from one of the folktales itself.

When the children had finished their food, the story was concluded until lunch the following day.

As Zeinab washed the plates, I asked who had told her the tale that she was retelling.

Thinking for a moment, she smiled at the corner of her mouth.

'My grandmother told me,' she said softly.

'And who told her?'

'Her grandmother, I suppose.'

I asked if Zeinab if had ever seen the story written down.

She balked at the thought of it.

'Of course not,' she said curtly.

'Why not?'

'Because spoken words are made of magic, rather than ink.'

Tahir Shah
Dar Khalifa

Tislit & the Seven Trials

Once upon a time, in the high valleys of the Atlas, there lived a wise and gentle girl named Tislit.

The daughter of a humble weaver, known throughout her village for her sharp mind and equally kind heart, Tislit carried a deep secret…

Her great abiding fear was failure.

She spent all her waking hours avoiding challenges, believing it was better to stay safe than to risk defeat.

One day, Idir, a respected village elder, called a gathering.

'The snows have fallen heavily this year,' he said gravely, 'and our food stores are running low. Someone must journey to the Sacred Cedar Grove to gather the healing bark that can nourish and protect us through the winter.'

The task was dangerous, for the Sacred Grove lay deep in the mountains, guarded by mysterious forces.

None dared to volunteer.

As silence fell over the crowd, Idir's piercing gaze landed on Tislit. 'You have a pure heart and the wisdom of the old ways,' he said. 'You are the one to go.'

Her heart racing, Tislit knew she could not refuse.

With her mother's blessing and a pouch of dried dates, she set off into the mountains.

Soon, she reached a roaring river.

Icy waters churned wildly, with no bridge in sight.

A voice from the water called, 'Turn back, child, or be swept away!'

Though terrified, Tislit remembered her father's words: 'Every thread has its place in the loom of life.' She gathered fallen branches, weaving them into a sturdy raft. With courage and determination, she crossed the river, leaving all doubts behind.

As night fell, Tislit sought shelter in a dark cave.

Inside, shadowy figures whispered, 'You are not strong enough for this journey.'

But Tislit knew the shadows were born of her own fears.

Closing her eyes, she sang an old lullaby her mother had taught her. The warmth of her song banished the shadows, and she slept peacefully.

At dawn, Tislit climbed a steep, icy path.

The wind howled, and her hands grew numb. Stumbling, nearly giving up, she followed the footprints of mountain goats.

She remembered her grandmother's advice: 'Follow the wisdom of nature.'

By stepping carefully where the goats had trodden, she made her way safely through the pass.

At the peak, Tislit encountered the Spirit of the Mountain, a towering figure cloaked in mist. 'Prove your worth,' it commanded. 'What is the most precious gift a person can offer?'

Tislit thought of gold, jewels, and rare spices but shook her head. Then she answered, 'It is trust, for without it, none can truly give or receive.'

The spirit nodded and vanished, leaving behind a glowing stone to guide her path.

Descending into a valley, Tislit heard voices mocking her: 'Turn back, little girl! You are too weak!'

This time, she did not falter. She shouted back, 'You are echoes, nothing more! My journey is my own, and I will not be swayed.'

The valley fell silent, and Tislit pressed on.

At last, she reached the Sacred Cedar Grove.

But, suddenly, seven majestic lions blocked her path.

Roaring, the great animals shook the ground.

Kneeling, Tislit addressed them:

'Great guardians, I come not to take but to share,' she said. 'My people need your bark to survive, but we will protect this grove in return.' The lions, sensing her sincerity, stepped aside.

With her pouch filled with the sacred bark, Tislit began her journey home. She faced the same challenges, but this time, she knew she was stronger.

When she finally returned to her village, she was greeted as a hero.

From that day on, Tislit became a symbol of courage and wisdom throughout the Atlas Mountains. Her story taught an important lesson, that true strength lies not in avoiding trials but in facing them with an open heart and a clear mind. For, only by confronting our fears, can we ever hope to be of service to others, and to discover ourselves.

Tarek & the Spell of Flight

In a peaceful village a day and a half on foot from Azrou, there once lived a curious and restless young man who went by the name of Tarek.

Although known for his cleverness, he rushed headlong into things without understanding their consequences.

He dreamed of escaping the limits of his small village, of soaring like the hawks that circled above, free and unbound by earthly cares.

One evening, as Tarek was sweeping his modest room, his broom knocked against a loose wooden plank beneath his bed.

Intrigued, he prised it open and discovered a dusty scroll wrapped in faded silk. Excited, he unrolled the scroll and saw strange symbols and words written in a flowing script.

At the bottom was a single line:

'Soar upwards on the wings of eagles, but beware the dangers of flight!'

Tarek's heart raced as he realized it was a magician's spell, one offering the ability to enable mortals to fly.

Throwing caution to the wind, he was gripped by the rawest sense of excitement he had ever known.

That very night, under the glow of a crescent moon, Tarek climbed to the highest hill outside the village. Standing tall, and clutching the scroll tightly, he recited the words as best he could.

At first, nothing happened.

But then, a sidewards gust of wind lifted him off the ground.

His mind reeling, he soared into the night sky.

As he flew high above the mountains, and his own village far below, Tarek cried out in wonder and awe.

Yet, as he tried to control his flight, the winds grew ferocious.

The sky darkening, he was thrown about like a dry leaf in a storm.

Crashing into thorn bush, his clothes were torn, his body badly bruised.

An ancient shepherd had observed that last moments of flight, and the arduous landing. Having lived through his share of adventures in distant lands, he approached Tarek and offered his advice:

'Surely, you must have misread the spell,' he said.

Determined to succeed, Tarek studied the scroll all the following night by candlelight, convinced he could master its spell.

Next morning, he tried again, this time reciting the words with more confidence.

Right away, he was hurled up into the sky, as though an eagle was carrying him on its wings.

At first, everything seemed perfect.

Tarik soared gracefully up, up, up, over the village, thrilling the onlookers below.

But as he climbed higher, the sun grew unbearably hot, and the spell faltered.

Tarek plummeted downwards through the blue sky, splashing down in the river.

Refusing to give up, he tried again and again, as he realised that it wasn't merely the words of the spell, but way they were spoken.

Each time he ascended into the sky, it would begin well enough, but end in failure.

A number of times, Tarek almost lost his life.

One afternoon, he was carried away by a whirlwind, and was deposited atop a distant cedar tree.

Another time, he flew into a flock of birds, who pecked at him until he tumbled earthward, his fall being broken by a haystack.

Each failure left Tarik more frustrated.

Meanwhile, the villagers grew increasingly angry at the chaos his attempts to fly exacted on them. Crops were trampled, rooftops damaged, and livestock scattered during his dramatic escapades.

At last, Tarek approached Amalu, a village elder, for guidance. 'Why does the spell always fail me?' he asked, his voice filled with despair.

Amalu took the scroll and examined it closely.

'You are not reading with care,' he said. 'This spell is not about the words or how they are spoken. It demands a clarity of mind, and an inner purity. To fly, you must be a master of virtues, of humility, patience, and respect.'

In coming days, Amalu instructed Tarek how to improve himself.

Days turned to weeks.

With much self-improvement, Tarek found himself becoming someone quite different than he had been.

And, then, when Amalu saw the young man was ready, he schooled Tarek in how to recite the spell correctly, emphasizing the pauses and the rhythm of the words.

After many weeks, the elder saw that his pupil was ready.

'Remember,' he warned, 'flight is certainly not the right of Man. The skies are not yours to command. Treat the spell, and the opportunity they permit with respect.'

This time, Tarek recited the spell with due reverence.

Lifting into the air, he flew upwards, steady and in harmony with the wind.

For many hours, Tarek soared gently above the mountains, no longer fighting the elements but moving with them.

When he returned to the ground, the villagers cheered.

From that day on, Tarek used the spell sparingly. And, with time, he forgot about it altogether.

But, he spent his days teaching others the values that mastery of the spell had taught him – the importance of patience, respect, and inner understanding.

The villagers still pass down the tale of Tarek and the Spell of Flight from one generation to the next, a lesson that a thing of wonder may in actual fact be something quite different instead.

The Eye of the Future

Once upon a time, there lived a young woman named Lalla Afiya, well-known for her courage and her keen intuition.

She lived at a time and a place in which life was very, very hard.

The crops in the fields often failed, the rivers ran dry, and the villagers struggled to survive.

Despite these hardships, Lalla Afiya refused to give in to despair.

One day, as she herded her goats along the rocky paths, an old traveller stopped her. His eyes sparkled with a mysterious light and his voice was soft but commanding.

'Child,' he said, 'I have heard of your bravery. Far beyond these peaks lies the Cave of Time, where the Eye of the Future rests. Those who look into it can glimpse what lies ahead and use that knowledge to change their fate. But beware, for the Eye shows both truth and illusion, and its gift must be used wisely.'

Filled with hope for her struggling village, Lalla Afiya decided to seek the cave.

She prepared for her journey, taking only a small pouch of dates, a water skin, and her mother's talisman for protection.

The path to the Cave of Time was perilous. Lalla Afiya climbed the steep cliffs, crossed the roaring rivers, and braved howling winds.

Along the way, she faced three trials:

First, she came upon a narrow, crumbling bridge spanning a vast chasm. As she stepped onto it, a voice whispered, 'Turn back now, because you are destined to fail.'

Lalla Afiya closed her eyes and whispered, 'Courage is my guide,' and crossed the bridge safely.

Second, the valley was filled with eerie whispers that spoke of her fears and insecurities. Lalla Afiya hummed a song her mother used to sing, drowning out the whispers until she reached the other side.

Lastly, at the entrance of the cave, she encountered a gate with two doors: one was marked 'Truth' and the other was marked 'Desire.' She hesitated but chose the door of 'Truth', believing her purpose was to help her village, not satisfy personal wants.

Inside the cave, the air shimmered with a golden glow. At its centre was a pedestal, upon which rested the Eye of the Future – a perfectly round, radiant orb that pulsed with light.

Approaching, Lalla Afiya gazed into the Eye.

At first, the visions were blurred, but soon they became clear. She saw her village flourishing, fields green with crops, and rivers flowing abundantly.

But she also saw shadows of conflict – villagers arguing over land, greed rising among them.

The Eye whispered, 'The future is never certain, young one. It bends to the will of those who act with wisdom or folly. Use this knowledge well.'

Lalla Afiya returned to her village and shared what she had seen. She urged the villagers to prepare for a prosperous harvest but warned them to remain united and humble.

They listened, and when the rains came, the fields blossomed as in her vision.

However, as prosperity grew, so did greed and envy.

Fights broke out over water rights, and old feuds were rekindled. Lalla Afiya, remembering the shadows she had seen, gathered the elders and spoke:

'The Eye of the Future showed me not only our blessings but also the dangers of division. If we are to thrive, we must share our abundance, and work together as one family.'

Lalla Afiya's words reminded the villagers of their shared struggles and the importance of unity. They mended their disputes and created new traditions to ensure fairness and cooperation.

The village prospered for generations, guided by Lalla Afiya's wisdom and the lessons of the Eye. It is said that she never looked into the Eye again, for she believed the true power of the future lay in the choices made in the present.

To this day, the tale of Lalla Afiya and the Eye of the Future is still told and retold –teaching those with the wisdom to listen that, while foresight can guide us, it is respect, unity, and the honouring of others that shape a brighter tomorrow.

The Golden Hen

In a small village set on the edge of the fertile valleys below Toubkal, there lived a poor widow named Hiba and her young son, Omar.

They owned only a few chickens and a tiny plot of land, but Hiba's gentle spirit and Omar's lively curiosity made them loved by the villagers. Despite their hardships, they always shared what little they had, believing that generosity and kindness were the greatest treasures.

One day, while Omar tended to the chickens, he noticed something extraordinary. One of their hens, a small, unassuming bird with feathers as white as snow, laid an egg unlike any he had ever seen – it glowed with a golden hue.

Startled, Omar ran to his mother, clutching the egg.

'Mother, look! The hen has laid a golden egg!'

Examining the egg, Hiba's hands were trembling.

'This must be a blessing,' she said. 'We will take it to the village elder for guidance.'

The village elder, Amghar, was wise and kind. When he saw the golden egg, he said, 'This hen is no ordinary bird. It is a gift from the spirits of the land, a reward for your generosity and pure hearts. But beware – this treasure must be used wisely, for greed can bring ruin even to the most blessed.'

Thanking Amghar, Hiba and Omar returned home.

From that day on, the hen laid a golden egg every morning.

Hiba sold the eggs, and used the money to repair their modest home and help the villagers, providing food, clothing, and tools for those in need. Their lives improved, but they remained humble, sharing their blessings with all.

However, news of the golden hen spread beyond the village, reaching the ears of a wealthy and ruthless merchant named Harun.

Envious of Hiba's newfound fortune, he devised a plan to steal the hen.

One moonless night, the merchant crept into Hiba's coop and snatched the golden hen. Cackling with laughter, he fled, imagining the endless riches the chicken would bring him.

The next morning, Hiba and Omar were heartbroken to find their beloved hen missing. They searched the village, but no one had seen it.

Omar said, 'Mother, I fear someone has stolen her.'

Meanwhile, Harun locked the hen in a golden cage and eagerly waited for it to lay an egg. But the hen refused. Day after day, the greedy merchant grew angrier, shouting at the bird and offering it luxurious food, yet it remained silent.

Frustrated, Harun cried, 'Why won't you lay your golden eggs for me?!'

The hen finally spoke, her voice soft but resolute. 'I lay golden eggs only for those with kind and generous hearts. Your greed has bound me, and so I will not lay any eggs.'

Realizing he could gain nothing from the hen, Harun abandoned the chicken in the mountains, hoping she would be lost forever.

One morning, as Omar searched the hills near their home, he heard a faint clucking. Following the sound, he found the golden hen nestled in a thicket. Overjoyed, he gently carried her back to the village. When the hen saw Hiba, she clucked happily and laid another golden egg, as if to celebrate her return.

From then on, the hen resumed giving her daily gift.

Having enough wealth to fulfil their own needs, Hiba and Omar sold the eggs and used the money to help others.

And, even though the villagers did not know it, at least half of the funds raised from the golden eggs was used to assist others anonymously.

The tale of Hiba and the Golden Hen reminds us all that true wealth lies not in material possessions, but in selflessness. Greed, like a barren field, yields nothing, while kindness and humility bring abundance and joy to all.

Tahar & the Little Sparrow

Once upon a time, in a secluded village, there lived an elder named Tahar, whose wisdom was sought by all.

Humble by nature, and treating everyone with respect – whether they were young or old, wealthy or poor – Tahar believed that respect was the thread which held the community together.

One afternoon, a proud and wealthy merchant named Harun arrived in the village, boasting of his travels and riches. He mocked the villagers for their simple ways, dismissing their traditions as outdated.

When he saw Tahar humbly sharing bread with a shepherd, he scoffed, 'What wisdom could ever come from a man who dines with peasants?'

Smiling gently, Tahar replied, 'Respect, like the sun, shines equally on all.'

Harun laughed and said, 'What can respect give you that wealth cannot?'

'Come to the Cedar Grove at dawn, and I will show you,' said Tahar, his eyes twinkling.

The next morning, Harun found Tahar sitting beneath a great cedar tree.

Chirping softly, a dainty little sparrow hopped up close to the elder's feet.

Tahar turned to Harun and said, 'This little sparrow holds the answer to your question. Watch and learn.'

Scattering crumbs on the ground, the elder spoke gently in the little bird's direction.

The sparrow hopped closer, pecking at the crumbs, its trust in the elder evident.

Harun frowned. 'What does a sparrow have to do with respect?'

Tahar smiled. 'If you wish to understand, try feeding it yourself.'

Impatient and brusque, Harun tossed down a handful of crumbs toward the sparrow and yelled, 'Come, bird, eat!'

Startled by Harun's tone, the sparrow fluttered away to a higher branch.

'You see,' Tahar said, 'respect is like the crumbs I offered. When given gently and sincerely, it builds trust and harmony. But when forced or laced with arrogance, it drives others away – even the smallest among us.'

Still sceptical, Harun challenged Tahar.

'Words are easy,' he said. 'Let us see if respect can achieve what wealth cannot.'

Nodding, Tahar led Harun to a nearby field where the village's water source flowed – a sacred spring that the villagers shared equally. The spring's guardian, an ancient tortoise named Tamimt, was said to appear only to those whose hearts were pure.

Harun, confident in his charm, approached the spring. 'I am Harun, a great merchant. Show yourself, Tamimt, and grant me the spring's blessings!'

The water rippled, but the tortoise did not appear. Frustrated, Harun turned to Tahar. 'Your tales are empty. This spring yields no secrets!'

Tahar knelt by the water, cupping his hands as he whispered, 'O Tamimt, guardian of life, I honour your presence and humbly seek your wisdom.'

The ripples grew into gentle waves, and from the depths emerged Tamimt, her shell glinting in the sunlight.

She spoke in a soft, measured voice, 'Tahar, your respect nurtures the village, like rain to the earth. You understand the balance of life.'

Turning her head to Harun, she said, 'Respect is not commanded; it is earned through humility and kindness. Until you learn this, the treasures of life will remain hidden from you.'

Humbled by Tamimt's words, Harun realized the error of his ways. He knelt before Tahar, admitting his arrogance and asking for forgiveness.

From that day, Harun stayed in the village, learning the ways of respect and humility. He became a generous benefactor, using his wealth to build new wells and a school, earning the love and admiration of the community.

The villagers still pass down the tale of Tahar and the Little Sparrow, which teaches us that respect is the foundation stone of harmony and trust. And they remind one another that, no matter how elevated one's status, it is respect – be it for human, animal, or even the smallest sparrow – that matters most of all.

Yassin, the Serpent, & the Magician's Box

South of the great mountains, and far inland from the ocean, a young man named Yassin once lived on the very edge of the Sahara's sands.

A humble shepherd, he spent his days guiding his flock through rocky hills and arid plains. Yassin was known for his curiosity, often wandering far beyond the village, dreaming of hidden wonders.

One morning, while resting beneath an old argan tree, Yassin heard a faint rustling in the brush. He turned to see a magnificent serpent, its scales gleaming like emeralds under the sun. The serpent was unlike any he had ever seen, its eyes sharp and filled with ancient wisdom.

The serpent spoke in a deep, melodic voice, 'Young shepherd, I have been cursed by a wicked magician. I am trapped in this form, and only one who possesses a brave heart and a pure soul can free me.'

Yassin, though startled, asked, 'What must I do to break your curse?'

'You must find the magician's box of magic,' the serpent explained. 'It is hidden deep within the Cave of Whispers. Inside, you will find the key to my freedom. But beware, for the magician has placed many traps to guard it.'

Yassin, determined to help the serpent, set out on his journey. He followed the serpent's guidance, crossing treacherous dunes, navigating thorny ravines, and enduring scorching winds. After days of travel, he finally reached the mouth of the Cave of Whispers, a dark and forbidding place where the wind seemed to carry voices from another world.

As Yassin stepped inside, he was greeted by a series of challenges:

First, Yassin faced a towering wall that shifted and twisted like living smoke. The shadows taunted him with his fears and doubts. Remembering the serpent's faith in him, Yassin steadied his heart and walked through the shadows, emerging unscathed.

Next, Yassin encountered a shimmering river that showed visions of his deepest desires – wealth, power, and a life of ease. Tempted but resolute, he refused to wade into the waters, knowing his task was far greater than selfish dreams.

Lastly, in the final chamber, Yassin heard whispers in every direction, urging him to turn back. 'The magician's power is too great,' they hissed. But Yassin closed his eyes, focused on the serpent's plea, and pressed on.

At the heart of the cave, Yassin found a pedestal upon which rested a small, ornately carved box. Symbols of the moon, stars, and serpents adorned its surface, and it pulsed with a faint, otherworldly glow.

Yassin hesitated, but a voice within him urged, 'The brave must act without fear.' He lifted the box, and the cavern began to shake. As the walls trembled, Yassin ran, clutching the box tightly. Just as the entrance collapsed behind him, he leapt to safety.

When Yassin returned to the argan tree, the serpent coiled around him in gratitude. 'You have done what few would dare,' it said. 'Open the box, and let its magic flow.'

Yassin opened the box, and a dazzling light burst forth, enveloping the serpent. Its emerald scales dissolved, revealing a young man dressed in royal robes.

'I am Idris, a prince of the desert,' the man said. 'The magician cursed me to live as a serpent after I refused to use his dark magic for harm. You have not only freed me but also broken his hold over my kingdom.'

As a reward, Idris gave Yassin a small pouch filled with enchanted seeds. 'Plant these, and your village will never know hunger again,' Idris said. 'You have proven that true strength lies in kindness and courage.'

Yassin returned to his village, where he planted the seeds. They sprouted into lush fields of grain and fruit-bearing trees, transforming the arid land into a fertile oasis. The villagers hailed Yassin as a hero, and his tale became a cherished legend.

From that day forward, the village told the story of Yassin, the Serpent, and the Magician's Box, teaching that bravery and a selfless heart can break even the darkest curses and bring light to all.

The Tale of
Tasnin & Amar

In the lush valleys of the Middle Atlas Mountains, where ancient cedar trees stretched their branches toward the heavens, there lived two neighbouring families.

One clan, the Ait Yidir, were shepherds, their flocks grazing on the high pastures.

The other, the Ait Zayd, were farmers, their fields bursting with barley and figs. Though both families lived side by side, they had long been at odds, their disputes over land and water stretching back for generations.

In the midst of this feud, Tasnin, the radiant daughter of the Ait Yidir, and Amar, the kind-hearted son of the Ait Zayd, met by chance in the cedar grove that marked the boundary of their families' lands. Tasnin had gone to gather wild herbs, and Amar was there to collect firewood. When their eyes met, it was as if the wind itself paused to listen to their hearts.

From then on, Tasnin and Amar met secretly in the grove, beneath the great cedar known as Ajdir al-Houb – the Cedar of Love. They shared stories, laughter, and dreams of a life free from the hatred that divided their families. Amar would weave her garlands of wildflowers, and Tasnin would sing songs that echoed through the trees like the murmur of a hidden spring.

Their love grew stronger with each passing day, but they knew their families would never allow them to marry. The Ait Yidir and Ait Zayd held tightly to their grudges, unwilling to forgive the wrongs of the past.

One evening, Tasnin's younger brother, suspicious of her frequent trips to the grove, followed her and discovered the lovers. Furious, he ran back to the Ait Yidir and revealed what he had seen. The news spread quickly, and both families were enraged.

'This is a betrayal of our honour!' shouted Tasnin's father.

'Our enemies will not take what belongs to us!' cried Amar's uncle.

The two families gathered under the moonlight, armed with their sharpest words and deepest resentments.

Determined to end the feud and prove their love, Tasnin and Amar stepped forward, hand in hand. Amar spoke first: 'Our love is like the cedar, rooted deeply in the earth. It does not bend to hatred or fear. If you wish to tear us apart, you must first destroy this grove, for it is where our souls meet.'

Tasnin added, her voice steady and clear: 'We ask for a chance to unite our families, to end the bitterness that has poisoned our hearts for too long. If we fail, then let the mountains themselves bear witness to our love.'

Moved by their courage, the village elder, who had long hoped for peace, stepped forward. 'The Cedar of Love has stood for centuries, sheltering us from storms and offering shade in the heat. Let these two young souls teach us what we have forgotten: that love is stronger than any feud.'

The elder proposed a test: beneath the Cedar of Love, Tasnin and Amar must each carve a symbol of their love into its trunk. If the cedar withstood the carvings without losing its strength, it would be a sign that their love was blessed by the spirits of the land, and the families would be bound by the cedar's enduring strength.

Tasnin carved a heart encircling two stars, and Amar carved a crescent moon embracing the sun. As they worked, the families watched in silence, their animosity momentarily softened by the couple's devotion.

When the carvings were complete, a gentle breeze swept through the grove, and the cedar seemed to shimmer under the moonlight. Not a single branch wavered, and its roots stood firm, as if to say, 'Love endures.'

The elder declared the cedar's blessing, and the families, humbled by the ancient tree's strength, agreed to set aside their differences. Tasnin and Amar's love became the bridge that united the Ait Yidir and Ait Zayd, and their wedding was celebrated beneath the Cedar of Love, with songs and dances that echoed through the valley.

From then on, the cedar grove became a place of peace and reconciliation, where couples would carve their own symbols of love into the ancient tree. And though Tasnin and Amar grew old, their love remained as steadfast as the great cedar, reminding the village that love, like the strongest tree, could weather even the fiercest storms.

Thus, certain people of the Middle Atlas recount the tale of Tasnin and Amar, as a lesson that love and forgiveness can heal even the deepest wounds.

The Tale of
Ayyad & the Hidden Treasure

Once upon a time, long ago, there lived in the shadow of the mountains, a simple farmer whose name was Ayyad.

Owning no more than a little plot of land, he toiled from sunrise to sunset, growing barley and tending his olive trees. Despite his hard work, his harvests were always meagre, and he barely had enough to feed himself and his family.

One year, a terrible drought struck the region.

The rivers dried up, the fields turned to dust, and Ayyad's crops withered under the relentless sun. Desperate and weary, Ayyad fell to his knees in the middle of his field and prayed:

'Great spirits of the earth, show me a way to provide for my family. I have given all my strength to this land, yet it gives so little in return. Please, help me.'

That night, Ayyad had a strange and vivid dream. In it, a figure cloaked in white appeared and said, 'Beneath your field lies a treasure of immeasurable worth. To find it, you must dig where the olive tree casts its shadow at midday. But beware, the treasure will not reveal itself to a heart filled with greed.'

When Ayyad awoke, he dismissed the dream as a trick of his weary mind. Yet, as the day wore on, the memory of the figure's words nagged at him. Finally, as the sun reached its peak, Ayyad stood beneath his ancient olive tree and began to dig where its shadow fell.

Hour after hour, Ayyad dug, the dry earth crumbling beneath his hands. Just as the sun began to set, his shovel struck something hard. His heart raced as he unearthed a heavy chest, its iron hinges rusted with age. He pried it open to reveal a dazzling collection of gold coins, jewels, and ancient artifacts that sparkled like stars.

Ayyad's first thought was to run back to the village and share his discovery, but a shadow of doubt crossed his mind. 'What if I keep this treasure for myself?' he wondered. 'I could live like a king and never toil again.'

Yet, as he gazed at the treasure, he felt a pang of guilt. He remembered the figure's warning: the treasure will not reveal itself to a heart filled with greed.

Ayyad decided to test the dream's truth. He took a handful of gold coins and used them to buy food and water for his village, which was suffering from the drought. He also repaired the village's broken well and shared the remaining food with those in need.

To his astonishment, the next day when he returned to the field, the chest was filled again, just as it had been before. This time, he took jewels to trade for seeds and tools, which he distributed among the villagers so they could replant their fields. Again, the chest replenished itself the following day.

News of Ayyad's generosity spread far and wide, and people from distant villages came to learn of his miraculous treasure. But Ayyad always told them the same thing: 'This treasure is not mine alone; it belongs to the earth and to those who respect its gifts. The more I share, the more it gives.'

In time, the drought ended, and the fields of Tazrout flourished like never before. Ayyad's treasure chest remained beneath the olive tree, a symbol of the power of selflessness and community. It was said that the chest would continue to give for as long as Ayyad and his descendants used its riches to help others.

The villagers of Tazrout passed down the tale of Ayyad and the Hidden Treasure for generations. They taught their children that true wealth is not in gold or jewels, but in the strength of a united and generous community. And so, the spirit of the treasure lived on, not only in the chest beneath the olive tree but in the hearts of the people who knew its story.

The Tree of Dying Stars

Once, when the mountains were little more than hills, and the rivers were no more than young streams glinting in sunlight, there lived a young shepherd named Amnay.

Known for his gentle heart and his songs, which echoed through the hills, he delighted in respecting his family and in his duty to tending the flock. Yet, beneath his songs lay a deep sorrow, for his parents had passed away during a harsh winter, leaving him alone in the world.

Amnay clung to hope, believing that his fortunes would one day change. But as the seasons turned and his life remained a lonely cycle of herding and solitude, his hope began to fade. His songs grew quieter, his heart heavier, until one day he stopped singing altogether.

One evening, as Amnay sat by his fire beneath the stars, a shadow appeared on the horizon. A cloaked traveller approached, leaning heavily on a staff. 'Peace be upon you,' the traveller said.

'And upon you, peace,' Amnay replied, offering the traveller bread and water.

The traveller studied the shepherd's tired eyes and asked, 'Why does your spirit sag like a branch burdened with too much fruit?'

'I have lost hope,' Amnay confessed. 'I once believed in brighter days, but they never came. My heart is as empty as the desert.'

The traveller nodded solemnly and said, 'There is a place called the Tree of Dying Stars, where those who have lost hope may seek answers. It lies deep in the Desert of Winds, beyond the shifting sands. But beware: the journey is perilous, and few return.'

Amnay, desperate to reignite his hope, resolved to find the tree. Setting off the next morning, he was guided by the traveller's instructions. His journey took him across scorching dunes, over jagged cliffs, and through valleys where the wind sang mournful songs. Along the way, he faced three trials:

First, Amnay entered a valley where every sound he made returned as a distorted, mocking echo. 'Why continue, shepherd of despair?' the echoes taunted. Amnay clenched his fists and pressed on, determined to find the tree despite the doubt that clawed at him.

Then, in a hidden oasis, Amnay came upon a pool whose surface reflected images of the life he had longed for – his parents alive, a loving family, and a prosperous home. The vision tugged at his heart, but he whispered, 'Illusions cannot fill an empty soul,' and walked away.

Finally, nearing the end of his journey, Amnay was caught in a blinding sandstorm. Dark shapes swirled around him, whispering his fears and regrets. He dropped to his knees, but a faint memory of his mother's voice urging him to endure gave him strength. He stood and walked forward, step by step, until the storm faded.

At last, Amnay reached the Tree of Dying Stars, a gnarled and ancient tree whose branches stretched toward the heavens, adorned with dim, flickering lights. The air around it was silent, heavy with the weight of lost hopes.

As Amnay approached, the largest star on the tree dimmed and fell at his feet, shattering into a thousand shards of light. A soft, melodic voice emerged from the shards:

'Amnay, hope is not a treasure that you lose; it is a seed that must be tended. Even in the darkest night, the smallest light can guide you forward. You journeyed here not to find hope, but to learn that hope must be carried within, even when the path is shrouded in shadow.'

The shards melted into the ground, and from the earth sprouted a small, glowing seedling. Amnay knelt and cradled it in his hands, feeling a warmth he had forgotten.

Amnay returned to his village, planting the seedling near his home. As it grew, its light brought life and warmth to the village, and people from distant lands came to see the miraculous tree. Amnay's songs returned, richer and more beautiful than ever, and although he still faced life's hardships, he no longer despaired.

Some people of this region still say that the Tree of Dying Stars continues to grow, its light a beacon for those who feel lost. Its tale reminds them that while hope may waver, it can never truly die, so long as one chooses to nurture it.

The Weaver
& the Endless Thread

In a remote village perched as it was on the edge of the Sahara, there once lived a weaver named Aqqa, known for her expertise in weaving.

From dawn until dusk, her loom clattered away, her hands moving so swiftly that she could finish more carpets in a day than any other weaver in the village. Yet, her carpets were plain and thin, and their threads often unravelled after a season of use.

In the same village lived Tamazirt, another weaver. Tamazirt worked slowly, her loom whispering softly as she wove intricate patterns into thick, durable carpets. Though she produced far fewer pieces than Aqqa, her carpets adorned the homes of chiefs and travellers who admired their beauty and strength.

In the grace of time, news spread that the sultan was seeking the finest carpet in the land. He announced a competition: the weaver who presented him with the best carpet would be granted a place in his court and a chest of gold.

Aqqa saw her chance to finally surpass Tamazirt. 'What use is one fine carpet,' she scoffed, 'when I can deliver a dozen to the sultan?' She set to work immediately, weaving day and night, her loom singing a relentless rhythm.

Tamazirt, as always, worked slowly and with great care. She chose her threads thoughtfully, dyeing them with natural pigments and weaving patterns that told the stories of her ancestors.

On the day of the competition, the sultan arrived with his entourage. Aqqa proudly presented twelve brightly colored carpets. Their sheer quantity dazzled the villagers, who murmured in admiration.

Tamazirt presented a single carpet, its intricate patterns shimmering like sunlight on sand. The sultan studied both weavers' work carefully, then spoke:

'Aqqa, your carpets are many, but their threads are loose, and their colors already fade. They will not last the season. Tamazirt, your single carpet is strong and tells the tale of your people. It will endure for generations. You, Tamazirt, are the winner.'

The villagers cheered, but Aqqa burned with anger and humiliation.

Determined to prove the sultan wrong, Aqqa loaded her loom onto a camel and journeyed into the desert, seeking the wisdom of the wind. She set up her loom among the dunes, challenging herself to weave the longest carpet the world had ever seen. She worked tirelessly, feeding her loom with thread after thread, until her carpet stretched farther than her eyes could see.

But as she worked, a great sandstorm rose from the horizon. The wind howled, and the sand tore through her endless carpet, reducing it to threads that vanished into the storm. Exhausted, Aqqa fell to her knees and cried, 'Why do my efforts amount to nothing?'

The wind softened and whispered, 'Quantity without quality is like sand without water – it cannot hold its shape. To create something lasting, you must weave with purpose, not pride.'

Humbled, Aqqa returned to her village. She approached Tamazirt and asked to learn her craft. Tamazirt welcomed her warmly, teaching her the art of weaving with patience, care, and meaning.

In time, Aqqa's carpets became as beautiful and enduring as Tamazirt's, and together they passed their knowledge to the next generation. The village thrived, and its carpets became legendary, valued not for their number but for the stories they told and the lives they touched.

Thus, the Amazighs of the village tell the tale of Aqqa the Weaver and the Endless Thread, reminding each other that the worth of what we create lies not in its abundance, but in its heart and purpose.

The Mountain of Forgiveness

Once upon a time, beneath the brooding glow of the moon, and the dazzling radiance of the sun, there lived in the Atlas Mountains a proud young man named Tazrart.

Although regarded for his sharp wit and unyielding pride, he often sought to elevate himself at the expense of others. A flaw in his character was his refusal to admit wrongdoing, even when his actions hurt those around him.

One day, Tazrart quarrelled with an elder named Amastan, a man revered for his wisdom and kindness.

In a fit of anger, the young man accused him of hoarding the village's blessings, and spread false rumours that turned some of the younger villagers against him.

Though Amastan said nothing, his silence carried the weight of disappointment, and the village's once harmonious spirit grew cold and divided.

That night, Tazrart dreamed of a towering, snow-capped mountain, shimmering in moonlight. A commanding voice spoke:

'You have sown discord where there was peace. To atone, you must climb the Mountain of Forgiveness and bring back the Stone of Truth. Only then will the village heal, and your heart find peace.'

When Tazrart awoke, he was gripped by both fear and determination. Without a word, he set off toward the mysterious mountain from his dream.

The path to the Mountain of Forgiveness was arduous, with steep cliffs, freezing winds, and narrow ledges. Along the way, Tazrart encountered three challenges, each forcing him to confront a part of himself he had long ignored:

First, Tazrart came to a swift, icy river with no visible way across. As he leaned over the water, he saw his reflection distorted and broken. The river whispered, 'To cross, you must see yourself clearly.' Tazrart knelt by the river and admitted, for the first time, that he had wronged Amastan and the village. As he spoke, the waters stilled, and a bridge of ice formed, allowing him to cross.

Then, beyond the river lay a dark forest, its twisted trees whispering fears and doubts. 'You are unworthy of forgiveness,' they hissed. Tazrart pressed on, repeating to himself, 'The journey itself is my penance.'

The shadows grew fainter as his resolve strengthened, and the forest opened to a sunlit path.

Finally, at the mountain's peak, Tazrart found a cave where a glowing stone lay atop an ancient altar. A voice echoed, 'To claim the Stone of Truth, you must decide: Do you seek forgiveness for your pride, or only to restore your standing?'

Tears filled Tazrart's eyes as he realized his deepest desire was to mend the harm he had caused, not for his own benefit, but for the village's peace.

With that revelation, he reached out and took the Stone of Truth. It was warm in his hands, and he felt its light seep into his heart.

Tazrart descended the mountain, the Stone of Truth glowing softly in his pouch. Upon returning to the village, he knelt before Amastan and confessed his lies, offering the stone as a symbol of his remorse.

Smiling, the elder and raised him to his feet, saying, 'True strength lies not in never faltering, but in the courage to make amends.'

The Stone of Truth was placed in the village square, where its light grew brighter each day, reminding all of the power of humility and forgiveness. Harmony returned to the village, and Tazrart became a man whose wisdom was sought by all.

Thus, the people of the village and of the valleys all around still tell the tale of Tazrart and the Mountain of Forgiveness, teaching that atonement requires both a journey of the heart and the courage to seek reconciliation.

The Singing Well

Long ago, deep in the gorges of the Draa Valley, there lived a young woman named Fariza, well-known throughout her village for her outward beauty.

Despite her physical looks, her heart had grown cold and the words she spoke were as sharp as thorns.

Having suffered greatly in her youth, losing both her parents to a harsh winter, Fariza had hardened herself against the world, believing kindness and love to be weaknesses.

One morning, as she wandered the hills, she came across an old shepherd sitting by a dry well. His face was lined with the wisdom of many years, and his eyes shone with a gentle light.

'Why do you sit by this barren well, old man?' Fariza asked curtly.

'This is no ordinary well,' the shepherd replied. 'It once sang with the purest water and could heal the deepest wounds. But its voice fell silent when greed and bitterness poisoned the land. Only a heart that has found redemption can bring it back to life.'

Fariza scoffed. 'Redemption is for the weak.'

The shepherd smiled and handed her a simple clay jug. 'Go to the Valley of Forgotten Tears and fill this jug with water from the hidden spring. But beware: the path is treacherous, and the spring only reveals itself to those who seek it with sincerity.'

Fariza, out of curiosity and a desire to prove the old man wrong, set off for the valley. Along the way, she encountered trials that tested her resolve. First, she crossed a raging river, where she saved a lamb stranded on a rock. Next, she climbed a steep cliff and helped an elderly woman gather firewood. Each act of kindness began to thaw the ice around her heart, though she refused to admit it.

Eventually, Fariza reached the Valley of Forgotten Tears, where she found a dry, cracked land. Exhausted and disheartened, she sat on a stone and wept for the first time since her parents' death. Her tears flowed freely, mingling with the dry earth. To her astonishment, the ground began to tremble, and a crystal-clear spring burst forth.

Fariza filled the jug and made her way back to the shepherd. When she poured the water into the dry well, a melodious song erupted, and the well overflowed with healing water. Villagers flocked to the well, their ailments cured, their hearts lightened.

The shepherd, now revealed as a spirit of the mountains, spoke to Fariza. 'Your journey has not only healed this land but also your heart. From this day forward, you will be a guide to those lost in bitterness and sorrow.'

Fariza returned to her village, her heart warm and her spirit renewed. She became a storyteller, sharing tales of redemption and hope, reminding all who listened that even the hardest hearts can learn to sing again. And so, the well continued to sing, its song a reminder that redemption is a journey worth taking, no matter how broken the path may seem.

The Tale of
Aksel & the Lion

In the shadow of the Tizi n'Test pass, where the soaring peaks of the High Atlas meet the vast plains, there lived a young warrior named Aksel.

Famed for his skill with the sword, Aksel was admired by one and all for his bravery.

But what really set him apart was his unwavering sense of chivalry.

Aksel believed that the strong should protect the weak, the wealthy should help the poor, and honour was worth more than gold. His mother often told him, 'True strength lies not in your sword, but in your heart.'

One day, word spread that a caravan travelling from Taroudant to Marrakech had been ambushed by a fierce lion. The beast had made its lair near a vital mountain spring, and without water, the travellers were stranded. The villagers whispered in fear, but Aksel stood tall.

'I will face the lion and free the spring,' he declared.

The elders tried to dissuade him, warning of the lion's ferocity. But Aksel simply said, 'Chivalry demands that I act, for the lives of many depend on this water.'

At dawn, Aksel rode up the steep mountain path, the sun casting long shadows over the rugged terrain. Near the spring, he found the lion – a huge creature with a golden mane, its roar echoing like thunder.

Aksel dismounted and approached cautiously, his sword drawn but his heart steady. The lion charged, but Aksel stood his ground, raising his shield to deflect the beast's mighty blows.

Then, remembering his mother's words, he lowered his sword and spoke calmly. 'Mighty lion, I do not seek to harm you. This spring is life to many. Let us share it, for the mountains belong to all.'

The lion paused, its fierce eyes locking with Aksel's. Slowly, it retreated to the shade of a nearby tree, as if recognizing the young warrior's courage and honour.

Aksel carefully cleared the stones blocking the spring, letting the water flow freely once more. He filled a leather pouch and left it near the lion, a gesture of respect.

When Aksel returned to the caravan and told his tale, the travellers rejoiced, and the elders marvelled at his bravery and wisdom. 'You faced the beast not with force, but with honour,' they said.

From that day forward, the story of Aksel and the Lion of Tizi n'Test became a legend, passed down through generations. It reminded the Amazigh people that true chivalry is not just about bravery, but also about respect, compassion, and using one's strength to serve others.

The Wisdom
of the Elderly Weaver

Long ago, in a little hamlet, nestled on the eastern flank of the Rif, there lived a skilled but aging weaver named Silya.

Her rugs were legendary, woven with patterns so intricate they seemed to tell the stories of the mountains and stars. Despite her frailty, the villagers often sought her wisdom, for Silya was said to possess knowledge handed down through generations.

Among the villagers was a young man named Idris, who dreamed of becoming the finest weaver in the region. Though talented, Idris was impatient and proud. He believed he had nothing to learn from an old woman whose hands trembled with age.

'She's had her time,' Idris told his friends. 'I'll surpass her soon enough.'

One day, the village chief announced a grand festival. As part of the celebration, a weaving competition would be held, and the winner's rug would be presented to the sultan himself. Idris saw his chance to prove his superiority.

Eager to win, Idris worked tirelessly on his rug, pouring all his energy into crafting the most vibrant colours and complex patterns he could imagine. One day, while tending to his loom, he noticed Silya sitting outside her home, watching the mountains.

'Why waste your time sitting idly, grandmother?' Idris called out. 'Surely you cannot compete in the festival with hands as shaky as yours.'

Silya smiled gently. 'Perhaps you are right, Idris. But even the oldest hands can still guide a thread through the loom.'

Idris laughed and returned to his work, convinced he had nothing to learn from her.

When the day of the festival arrived, the village square was adorned with bright banners, and the air buzzed with excitement. One by one, the weavers presented their rugs. Idris unveiled his masterpiece last, a stunning display of vivid colours and intricate designs. The crowd gasped in admiration, certain he would win.

But then Silya stepped forward, carrying a rug so simple it seemed plain compared to Idris's. The villagers murmured, puzzled by her choice.

The chief examined both rugs carefully. When he held up Idris's rug to the sunlight, the intricate designs began to unravel, the threads pulling loose. The young man's face fell as he realized his mistake: he had prioritized appearance over strength, rushing through the foundational weaving.

Next, the chief held up Silya's humble rug. Though its design was simple, its craftsmanship was flawless, each thread tightly bound. 'This rug will endure,' the chief declared. 'Its strength lies in its foundation, just as wisdom lies in respecting those who came before us.'

Idris hung his head, understanding the lesson too late.

After the festival, Idris approached Silya and bowed low. 'Grandmother, I was wrong to dismiss your wisdom. Will you teach me the secrets of your weaving?'

Silya smiled, her eyes twinkling like the stars she wove into her rugs. 'Respect and patience, Idris. These are the strongest threads of all.'

From that day forward, Idris became her apprentice, learning not just the craft of weaving but the deeper wisdom of humility and respect for elders. Together, they created rugs that told the stories of their people, each one stronger and more beautiful than the last.

And so, the people of the Rif passed down this tale, reminding each generation to honour the wisdom of their elders, for their guidance is the foundation upon which all great things are built.

The Tale of Yamina
& the Star of the Desert

Long ago, in a place whose name has been forgotten through the twists and turns of time, there lived a young girl named Yamina.

Popular with everyone else in the village, and beautiful beyond description, she spent her days weaving rugs, gathering water from the oasis, and helping her mother tend their modest garden.

Though her family was poor, she was always quick to share their humble meals with travellers and neighbours in need.

One evening, while returning from the well, Yamina saw an old woman sitting alone beneath a date palm. The woman's clothes were tattered, and her face was lined with years of hardship.

'Grandmother, are you hungry?' Yamina asked, kneeling beside her.

The old woman nodded, her voice barely a whisper. 'I have not eaten in days.'

Without hesitation, Yamina handed her the bread and figs she carried for her family's dinner. 'Take this, and may it give you strength.'

The old woman smiled. 'Bless you, child. Your kindness will light your path when you need it most.'

Yamina thought little of the words and hurried home, her heart light despite the empty basket.

A few nights later, a fierce storm swept through the valley, flooding fields and washing away homes. When the storm passed, the villagers discovered that their precious water from the oasis had vanished, swallowed by the desert sands. Without water, their crops would fail, and their livestock would perish.

Desperate, the village elders called a meeting. 'Someone must journey across the desert to find the source of a new spring,' one elder declared. 'It is a perilous journey, but without water, we will all perish.'

Yamina stood and spoke. 'I will go.'

Her mother gasped. 'No, Yamina! You are but a child, and the desert is treacherous.'

But Yamina's resolve was firm. 'If I can save our village, I must try.'

The next morning, Yamina set out at dawn, carrying only a small flask of water and her father's old staff. She walked for days, her feet sinking into the burning sands, her lips cracked and dry. Each night, she gazed at the stars, hoping they would guide her.

On the third night, a dazzling star appeared in the northern sky, brighter than any Yamina had ever seen. Its light seemed to shimmer and dance, leading her deeper into the desert. She followed it, her strength waning but her determination unshaken.

At last, she reached a hidden valley where a crystal-clear spring bubbled up from the rocks. Beside the spring stood a figure cloaked in golden robes, their face hidden by a veil.

'You have come far, Yamina,' the figure said, their voice as soft as the desert breeze. 'Why have you risked your life to find this spring?'

'For my village,' Yamina replied without hesitation. 'Our people will die without water.'

The figure nodded. 'You seek water for others, though you yourself are parched. This selflessness is rare. Drink, Yamina, and take this gift back to your people.'

Kneeling, she drank deeply from the spring.

As she did so, she sensed her strength returning.

When she rose, the figure was gone, but in their place lay a smooth, glowing stone. It pulsed with a soft, golden light, like the star that had guided her.

Yamina filled her flask and began the journey home, the glowing stone lighting her way through the darkness.

When she returned to the village, the people rejoiced, their hope renewed. Yamina poured the water from her flask onto the dry ground, and to everyone's astonishment, a new spring burst forth, its waters pure and plentiful.

The glowing stone, which Yamina placed at the spring's edge, became a symbol of the village's salvation. It was said that as long as the people remained selfless and shared their blessings, the spring would never run dry.

Yamina's tale was passed down through generations, a reminder of the power of selflessness. To this day, mothers still whisper the tale to their children, the tale of a brave girl who followed the star and brought life to her people, teaching them that true strength lies in giving without expecting anything in return.

The Tale of the
Generous Shepherd

Once upon a time, in the rocky foothills of the Atlas Mountains, there lived a young shepherd named Amrou.

Although very much like the other boys in the village, Amrou was especially well-regarded because of his extraordinary generosity.

Though he possessed only a small flock of sheep and a modest clay house, he shared what little he had with anyone in need, be it food, water, or shelter from the mountain winds.

One evening, as the sun dipped behind the peaks, Amrou herded his sheep to a grassy knoll near the sacred spring of Aïn Ifrane. The spring, said to be protected by an ancient djinn, was a place of both beauty and mystery.

As Amrou filled his waterskin, he noticed a frail old man sitting by the spring, shivering despite the warm breeze.

'Peace be with you, father,' Amrou greeted, offering his cloak. 'You seem cold and weary. Please take this to warm yourself.'

The old man smiled but said nothing. Amrou then handed him some bread and dates from his satchel. 'Eat, and may it give you strength.'

After eating in silence, the old man spoke in a voice that resonated like the wind through the canyons. 'You have given freely, though you have little. Such generosity will not go unrewarded.'

Before Amrou could respond, the man vanished, leaving behind only the faint scent of wild thyme.

The next morning, Amrou awoke to find a dazzling white ram among his flock. Its horns gleamed like silver, and its wool shimmered like the snows on the highest peaks. Though puzzled, Amrou welcomed the ram, believing it to be a blessing.

As the days passed, news of the magnificent ram spread throughout the region. One day, a poor farmer from a distant village arrived, pleading with Amrou. 'My children are starving, and my fields are barren. I have nothing to offer but my prayers. Could you spare a sheep to save my family?'

Without hesitation, Amrou gave the man one of his sheep. The farmer left with tears of gratitude, and that night, the white ram seemed to grow even more radiant.

But the true test came when a wealthy merchant, greedy and cunning, approached Amrou with a sly smile. 'That ram of yours is worth a fortune,' the merchant said. 'Sell it to me, and you'll never have to work another day in your life.'

Amrou shook his head. 'This ram is not for sale, for its value is not in gold but in the blessing it brings.'

The merchant scoffed and left in anger, but Amrou remained steadfast.

One evening, as Amrou rested by the spring, the old man appeared again, now clad in flowing robes that shimmered like moonlight. 'You have passed the test of true generosity,' the old man said, revealing his true form as the Djinn of the

Mountain. 'For your kindness and refusal to be swayed by greed, I will grant you a gift.'

With a wave of his hand, the djinn transformed Amrou's modest flock into a great herd of sheep, their wool as soft as clouds. He also blessed the spring so that it would never run dry, providing water for Amrou's flock and all who passed through the mountains.

'Remember,' the djinn warned, 'true wealth lies in a generous heart. Guard it well.'

From that day on, Amrou's herd thrived, and his village prospered. He shared his abundance with everyone, and travellers from far and wide came to drink from the spring and hear the tale of the generous shepherd who won the favour of the Djinn of the Mountain.

And so the people of the Atlas tell this story to remind each generation that the greatest treasure is found not in gold, but in the kindness we show to others.

The Journey
to the Singing Tree

Once upon a time, in the glorious valley of Oulrika, there lived two children, Tazgha and Amir.

Tazgha was as curious as a sparrow, always asking questions, while Amir, her best friend, was as brave as a lion, always ready for an adventure.

One morning, shortly after dawn, the village elder told a story of the Singing Tree, a magical tree that grew high in the mountains. Its leaves, when touched by the wind, sang songs that revealed ancient secrets and wisdom. The elder said the tree had stopped singing, and the people feared they would lose its blessings forever.

Tazgha's eyes sparkled with excitement. 'Let's find the Singing Tree!' she said. Amir hesitated for a moment but then nodded. 'We'll bring back its song,' he promised.

Early the next morning, Tazgha and Amir packed some bread, dates, and a flask of water. They set out at sunrise, following the elder's vague directions: 'Climb where the eagles soar, and seek the valley of a thousand stones.'

Their journey was filled with challenges. They crossed icy rivers, climbed steep cliffs, and faced howling winds. At one point, they encountered a stranded baby goat, trapped on a narrow ledge. Tazgha insisted they rescue it. With Amir's strength and Tazgha's quick thinking, they brought the goat to safety.

'Every life matters,' Tazgha said as the goat scampered away. Amir smiled. 'You're right.'

After three days, they reached the valley of a thousand stones. There, they found an old woman wrapped in a brightly woven cloak, sitting by a small fire.

'Who seeks the Singing Tree?' she asked in a raspy voice.

'We do,' Tazgha and Amir replied in unison.

The woman handed them a small clay jar. 'The tree has lost its song because the people have forgotten to listen. Fill this jar with water from the spring at the top of the mountain, and pour it at the tree's roots. But beware, the mountain tests all who climb it.'

With the jar in hand, they began their ascent. The mountain seemed to come alive, throwing challenges their way. A fierce storm rolled in, forcing them to take shelter in a cave. Inside, they found strange carvings on the walls – stories of their ancestors, who had once climbed the same mountain to seek the Singing Tree's wisdom.

As they rested, Amir confessed, 'I'm scared, Tazgha. What if we fail?'

Tazgha took his hand. 'Courage is not the absence of fear, but facing it together.'

Inspired, they pressed on and finally reached the spring. They filled the jar with crystal-clear water and hurried to the tree.

The Singing Tree stood tall and majestic, its branches twisted like the lines of an ancient script. Tazgha poured the water at its roots, and the tree began to hum softly. The hum grew into a melody, and then into a beautiful, haunting song.

In its music, they heard a message: 'Wisdom is not in the seeking but in the sharing. Care for each other, and care for the world, for all are connected.'

Tazgha and Amir felt the truth of these words in their hearts. They knew their journey was not just to restore the tree's song but to remind their people of the importance of unity, compassion, and listening.

When they returned to Tighremt, the entire village gathered to hear their story. Tazgha and Amir shared not only their adventure but also the Singing Tree's wisdom. From that day on, the village came together to care for one another and the land around them.

And so, the Singing Tree's song lived on, not just in its leaves but in the hearts of the people.

The Tale of the
Mechanical Horse

Long ago, beyond the cedar forests of Ifrane, there lived a brilliant inventor named Yazid.

Famed for crafting intricate tools, water mills, and even musical instruments that played by themselves, he dreamt of creating a horse that required no food or water, while travelling faster than the wind and yet never tire.

For years, Yazid worked tirelessly in his mountain workshop, hammering, carving, and shaping pieces of metal and wood. Finally, he succeeded. He had built a magnificent mechanical horse, its body gleaming like polished silver, its hooves clinking like small bells. The horse moved gracefully and obeyed every command as if it were alive.

The villagers marvelled at Yazid's creation, and even the tribal chieftain came to see it. 'Yazid,' the chieftain said, 'with this horse, you could travel to faraway lands, explore unknown places, and even win great riches. It is a marvel beyond compare.'

Yazid, proud of his invention, decided to embark on a journey to show the world his masterpiece. He rode the mechanical horse across deserts, through bustling cities, and over snow-capped mountains. Wherever he went, people admired the horse, offering him gold, jewels, and fine clothes in exchange for it. But Yazid always refused, saying,

'This horse is not for sale. It is a symbol of what human ingenuity can achieve.'

One bright afternoon, Yazid reached a distant kingdom ruled by a greedy sultan. The ruler, dazzled by the mechanical horse, demanded that Yazid sell it to him.

Politely, Yazid refused, explaining that the horse was not just a machine but a part of his soul.

The sultan grew furious and had Yazid imprisoned, intending to keep the horse for himself.

Locked in the sultan's dungeon, Yazid despaired. He realized he had become so consumed by pride in his creation that he had forgotten the true purpose of his work: to benefit others, not to seek fame or fortune.

Meanwhile, the sultan ordered his guards to ride the mechanical horse, but no one could control it. The horse bucked, reared, and finally galloped away, vanishing into the distant horizon. The sultan was left empty-handed, his greed punished by the very thing he sought to possess.

In his cell, Yazid reflected on his journey and vowed to change. One night, the mechanical horse returned, finding its way back to its creator. Its hooves clinked softly as it stood outside Yazid's cell. Inspired by its loyalty, Yazid used his ingenuity to escape and returned to his village.

Back in Ifrane, Yazid dismantled the mechanical horse and used its parts to build new tools and machines for the village – water pumps for the fields, mills for grinding grain, and even a loom that wove blankets to keep the villagers warm during the harsh winters. The villagers prospered, and Yazid became beloved not for his marvels but for his kindness and service.

Though the mechanical horse no longer roamed the lands, its spirit lived on in the improved lives of the people. Yazid had learned that the true value of his skill was not in impressing others but in lifting his community.

True greatness lies not in what you create for yourself, but in how your creations serve and uplift others.

The Lesson of the Stone

Once upon a time, nestled between rugged cliffs and vast desert sands, there existed a little farming town called Tissia.

The people lived in harmony with nature, and relied on the land for their survival – growing barley, raising sheep, and gathering water from a sacred spring hidden deep in the mountains. Believing the spring was a gift from Anzar, the Rain Spirit, they guarded it with great care.

One fateful night, a blazing streak of light tore across the dark sky. A meteor, glowing like a fragment of the sun, crashed into the desert not far from the village. Its impact shook the earth, and a brilliant, otherworldly stone remained at the crater's centre, pulsing with a strange, warm light.

Curious and frightened, the villagers gathered around the fallen star. The village elder, Tihya, warned them, 'This is no ordinary stone. It is a gift from the heavens, but we must discover its purpose before deciding what to do with it.'

Over the next few days, the villagers discovered that the meteor had extraordinary powers. When placed near water, it caused plants to grow faster and more abundantly. When touched by the sick or injured, it brought healing and renewed strength. The villagers began to call it the Tafoukt Stone, or the Stone of Light.

The people rejoiced, believing the stone could bring prosperity to the entire village. However, as word spread, greed began to creep into their hearts. Some villagers believed they should use the stone only for their own benefit, while others wanted to trade it for wealth and gold from distant lands.

One day, a drought struck the land, and the sacred spring began to dry up. The crops wilted, and the sheep grew weak. The villagers turned to the Tafoukt Stone, believing it could save them. But disagreements broke out: some wanted to use its power immediately, while others argued it should be saved for even greater emergencies.

The elder Tihya spoke gravely: 'The stone has been sent to test us, not to divide us. Its power is a gift, but if we use it selfishly, it will bring misfortune instead of blessings.'

Despite her warnings, a few villagers attempted to take the stone for themselves. That night, a violent storm descended upon the village, with winds howling and lightning striking the earth. The Tafoukt Stone glowed fiercely, and its light seemed to split into two: one half dimmed, while the other rose into the sky and disappeared.

When the storm passed, the villagers found the Tafoukt Stone had lost much of its power. Crops still grew, but no faster than before, and the sick could no longer be healed by its touch. Filled with regret, the villagers gathered around Tihya, who said, 'The stone's light returned to the heavens because we allowed greed and division to taint its gift. Let this be a reminder that blessings must be shared and cherished together, not hoarded or fought over.'

From that day on, the villagers worked together to protect their land and care for one another, learning to rely on their own strength and unity rather than magical aid. Though the

Tafoukt Stone remained in the village as a symbol of their lesson, its true power lay in the harmony it restored among the people.

The Magical Tarboush

Once upon a time, not too far from the almond trees and giant boulders of Tafraout, there lived a young man named Rahil.

Hailing from a family of weavers, he was known for his laziness and lack of ambition. He spent his days dreaming of a life filled with wealth and ease but did little to improve his circumstances.

One afternoon, while wandering aimlessly through the hills, Rahil stumbled upon a small, hidden cave. Inside, he found a dusty yet beautifully embroidered tarboush hat resting on a stone pedestal. Intrigued, he picked it up, and the moment he placed it on his head, he heard a deep, resonant voice.

'This is the Tarboush of Wisdom and Fortune,' the voice said. 'It will grant you one magical wish each day, but only if your heart is pure and your intentions are selfless.'

Excited, Rahil couldn't believe his luck. 'With this hat, I'll never have to work again!' he thought.

That evening, Rahil returned to the village and announced to himself, 'I wish for a grand feast fit for a king!' Instantly, a table laden with exotic dishes, golden platters, and sweet honey cakes appeared before him. Rahil ate to his heart's content, convinced that the tarboush was his key to an easy life.

But the next morning, he woke up to find the food gone, and the hat felt heavier on his head. The voice returned, warning him, 'The magic of this tarboush grows weaker with selfish wishes. Use it wisely.'

Rahil shrugged off the warning, determined to enjoy his newfound power.

The next day, as Rahil lounged under an almond tree, he noticed an old beggar shivering by the roadside. The man's clothes were torn, and his face was weathered by years of hardship. For a moment, Rahil thought of using his daily wish to help the beggar, but his greed got the better of him.

'I wish for a chest of gold coins!' Rahil declared, and the tarboush granted his wish. The chest appeared, heavy and shining, but the beggar's tired eyes stayed with him, filling him with unease.

That night, Rahil couldn't sleep. The tarboush now weighed so heavily on his head that it hurt his neck. The voice spoke again, sterner this time: 'True fortune comes not from hoarding wealth but from sharing it. Your wishes will only bring burden if your heart remains selfish.'

The next morning, Rahil saw a group of villagers gathered by the river. The only bridge leading to the village fields had collapsed, leaving their crops at risk of withering without water. Desperate, they tried to find a way to carry water across the rocky terrain.

For the first time, Rahil felt ashamed of his greed. He touched the tarboush and whispered, 'I wish for the bridge to be restored.'

In an instant, the bridge reappeared, stronger than before. The villagers cheered, and for the first time in his life, Rahil felt a sense of true fulfilment.

The tarboush grew lighter on his head, and the voice returned, now warm and approving. 'Your heart has begun to understand the value of giving.'

From that day on, Rahil used the tarboush to help his community. He wished for wells in dry seasons, tools for struggling farmers, and even books for the village children. Each act of generosity brought joy not only to the villagers but also to Rahil himself.

As the years passed, the Tarboush became lighter and lighter until, one day, it disappeared altogether. Rahil no longer needed its magic, for he had discovered that the greatest power lay in using his talents and resources to uplift others.

Rahil became a beloved leader, and his story was passed down through generations, teaching that true fortune comes from selflessness and kindness.

The Tale of the Treasure Map

Long ago, in the vast and golden sands of the Sahara, there lived a humble shepherd named Mustafa, who had been born and raised in the village of Aït Lahcen.

Mustafa was honest and hard-working, but he dreamed of a better life for his family. He longed to find wealth to ease their burdens, but he remained content with his simple life, tending to his goats and finding joy in the desert's quiet beauty.

One evening, as the sun dipped below the horizon, Mustafa noticed something unusual glinting in the sands near an ancient palm tree. He knelt down and uncovered a rolled piece of leather – a map, marked with symbols and strange writing. At the bottom, it bore the words: 'The Treasure of Tassili Awaits the Pure of Heart.'

Thrilled, yet cautious, Mustafa showed the map to the village elder, Tammouzt. The wise old man examined it and said, 'This map leads to Tassili, a hidden valley said to hold great treasures. But remember, Mustafa, treasure does not always mean gold. The journey will test your heart and your intentions.'

Determined to uncover the treasure, Mustafa set out the next morning. The map led him through scorching sands, jagged rocks, and narrow mountain passes.

Along the way, he encountered three travellers in need of help:

The first was a lost merchant struggling to find his way back to his caravan.

The second was an injured falcon trapped in a thorny bush.

The third was an old woman whose water jar had shattered, leaving her parched under the desert sun.

Though he was eager to reach the treasure, Mustafa paused each time to help. He guided the merchant to safety, freed the falcon, and gave the old woman his own water, despite his growing thirst.

Finally, after days of hardship, Mustafa reached the hidden valley of Tassili.

At its centre stood a solitary cave.

Following the map, he entered and found a small chest, its lid engraved with the same phrase: 'The Treasure of Tassili Awaits the Pure of Heart.'

When Mustafa opened the chest, he was surprised to find no gold or jewels, only an old, worn mirror. Confused and disappointed, he gazed into the mirror – and saw a reflection not of his face, but of all the kind deeds he had performed on his journey: the merchant safely reunited with his caravan, the falcon soaring freely in the sky, and the old woman drinking water from a fresh spring.

As he watched, the reflection shimmered, and the mirror spoke: 'True treasure lies in the goodness of your heart and the lives you touch. Your kindness has brought wealth beyond measure, for it enriches both you and the world around you.'

Mustafa returned to Aït Lahcen carrying the mirror, unsure of how the villagers would react to his story. To his surprise, they welcomed him with open arms, eager to hear of his journey. Inspired by his acts of generosity, the villagers began helping one another more freely, creating a community stronger and happier than ever before.

The merchant Mustafa had saved sent gifts of spices and goods to the village. The falcon often returned, guiding Mustafa and his flock to hidden oases. And the old woman blessed the village with her prayers, ensuring their fields remained fertile even in times of drought.

Mustafa had discovered not only the treasure of Tassili but also the true meaning of wealth: a life lived with compassion and selflessness.

The greatest treasures are found not in riches, but in the kindness we show to others and the love we build in our communities.

The Tale of the
Magic Coin

In the ancient village of Tiziri there lived a beggar named Amar.

Though he owned nothing but the tattered clothes on his back, his heart was kind and he was generous by nature. He often shared what little food he had with stray animals and helped villagers with small tasks in exchange for scraps of bread.

One day, as Amar wandered through the foothills searching for firewood, he stumbled upon a shiny object half-buried in the sand. It was a golden coin, etched with mysterious symbols and glinting in the sunlight. As he picked it up, an old man dressed in a flowing white robe appeared out of thin air.

'Amar,' the old man said, his voice gentle yet commanding, 'you have found the Coin of Abundance. With this coin, whatever you spend will return to you tenfold. But beware: its power is meant to help those in need, not to fulfil greed.'

Amar bowed and thanked the old man, who vanished as suddenly as he had appeared.

Excited yet cautious, Amar decided to test the coin. He went to the village market and bought a single loaf of bread, using the coin to pay. As he walked away, he felt a strange warmth in his pocket. Reaching in, he found not one, but ten golden coins! Overjoyed, Amar realized the coin's magic was real.

Instead of keeping the gold for himself, Amar began to buy food, clothes, and blankets for the poor. He distributed his newfound wealth among the villagers, ensuring that no one went to bed hungry or cold. The more he gave, the more the coin multiplied his generosity. The village prospered, and Amar became beloved by all.

Word of Amar's miraculous coin spread beyond Tiziri, reaching the ears of a wealthy merchant named Hammou. Driven by greed, Hammou devised a plan to steal the coin. He invited Amar to his grand home under the guise of gratitude, offering a feast in his honor.

During the feast, Hammou distracted Amar with stories of distant lands and secretly switched the coin with a plain one. That night, Hammou laughed triumphantly, holding the stolen coin in his hands. 'Now I will be the richest man in all the land!' he gloated.

Eager to test the coin's magic, Hammou went to the market and bought a luxurious robe. But when he checked his pockets, he found nothing but dust. Furious, he tried again, purchasing jewels and fine spices, yet the coin never returned its magic.

Meanwhile, Amar, unaware of the theft, continued his acts of kindness, using what little he had to help others. One day, as he sat by the village well, the old man in the white robe appeared once more.

'Amar,' the old man said, 'the coin was taken from you, but its magic remains with those who use it wisely. True abundance lies not in the gold itself, but in the generosity of your spirit. For this reason, the blessings you bring will never cease.'

At that moment, a stream of silver water bubbled from the ground where Amar sat. It flowed into the village, turning barren fields green and ensuring that no one in Tiziri would ever go thirsty again.

Hammou, now shunned by the villagers, returned the coin to Amar, hoping to regain his wealth. But Amar only smiled and said, 'The coin's power is not in its possession, but in its purpose. Use what you have to help others, and you will find true riches.'

Humbled by his experience, Hammou began to change. He used his wealth to repair the village's crumbling homes and supported Amar in his mission to care for the needy. Over time, he learned that the joy of giving far outweighed the fleeting satisfaction of greed. For, true wealth is not measured by what you keep, but by what you give to others with a sense of love in your heart.

The Mirror of Aksil

Once upon a time, in the distant climes of the Rif, there was a thriving village where the people lived simple yet content lives.

Among them was a young man named Aksil, who was admired for his striking looks and charm. But, his one flaw was his arrogance.

You see, he believed his beauty made him superior to others, and he often mocked those he deemed less fortunate.

One day, while wandering through the forest, Aksil came across a peculiar old shop hidden among the trees. Inside was a wrinkled merchant with a long, flowing beard and eyes that gleamed with wisdom. The merchant greeted him warmly and showed him his wares, but one object immediately caught Aksil's attention – a beautiful, silver-framed mirror.

'What makes this mirror so special?' he asked, running his fingers along the intricate patterns on the frame.

The merchant smiled knowingly. 'This is the Mirror of Truth. It shows not your outer appearance, but the true reflection of your soul.'

Intrigued and eager to see his inner beauty, Aksil bought the mirror and hurried home.

Once alone, Aksil gazed into the mirror, expecting to see an even more dazzling version of himself. But what he saw made his heart stop. Staring back at him was a hunched, shadowy figure with twisted features and hollow, sorrowful eyes. His reflection looked frail and broken, its hands trembling as if burdened by an invisible weight.

'This must be a trick!' Aksil shouted, throwing the mirror aside. But the image haunted him. No matter how many times he looked, the distorted figure remained.

Confused and angry, Aksil returned to the merchant and demanded an explanation.

'The mirror reveals the truth,' the merchant said calmly. 'Your outer beauty is a mask, hiding the selfishness and cruelty within. If you wish to change what you see, you must change your heart.'

Aksil was deeply troubled. He realized that while people admired his looks, few truly loved or respected him. Determined to change, he began to act with kindness. He helped the elderly carry water from the well, shared his food with the hungry, and spoke gentle words to those he once mocked.

At first, these actions felt foreign, but over time, Aksil found joy in seeing others smile. Slowly, his arrogance melted away, replaced by a genuine desire to do good.

Months later, Aksil gathered the courage to look into the mirror again. This time, the reflection was different. The shadowy figure had grown brighter, its hunched back straightened, and its eyes sparkled with warmth and compassion. Though still not perfect, the image radiated a quiet strength and peace.

Aksil smiled, understanding the merchant's words at last: the mirror had never been cursed – it had simply shown him the truth.

He decided to share the mirror's power with the villagers.

Placing it in the village square, he invited everyone to look into it.

At first, many were frightened or ashamed of their reflections, but Aksil encouraged them to see it as an opportunity for growth.

Over time, the village transformed. People became kinder, more patient, and more understanding of one another. The mirror became a symbol of self-reflection and inner transformation, and Aksil was no longer just admired for his beauty but loved for his character.

The Flying Carpet

In a tiny community a stone's throw from the sands of the great Sahara, there once lived a humble weaver named Imalou.

Renowned for the vibrant carpets she wove, each thread dyed with colours drawn from desert flowers, saffron, and indigo, her carpets were said to contain the whispers of the desert winds, and stories of faraway lands.

One day, while collecting herbs in a hidden valley, Imalou stumbled upon an old woman sitting by a dried-up spring. The woman's skin was weathered like the bark of an ancient tree, and her eyes sparkled like morning dew.

'Imalou,' the woman said, her voice soft yet commanding, 'I am Lalla Tiddukla, the guardian of this valley. You have a kind heart and skilled hands. In return for your goodness, I shall grant you a gift. Weave a carpet from the threads of your soul, and it will fly wherever your heart desires.'

Imalou bowed respectfully and returned home, her mind racing with the possibilities of such a gift.

For days and nights, Imalou worked tirelessly. She poured her hopes, dreams, and love for her people into every thread. The finished carpet shimmered like the desert under the moonlight, its intricate patterns seeming to shift and dance.

When Imalou stepped onto the carpet and whispered her wish, it rose gracefully into the sky. She soared above the sand dunes, over lush oases, and even to distant mountains. Her heart swelled with joy, knowing she could bring back stories, knowledge, and treasures to her village.

News of Imalou's flying carpet spread quickly, reaching the ears of a rich merchant named Taghazout. Greedy and cunning, he visited Imalou under the pretense of admiration for her work.

'This carpet could make you the richest woman in all the land,' Taghazout said. 'Sell it to me, and I will give you enough gold to live in luxury forever.'

Imalou shook her head. 'This carpet is not for wealth or pride; it is meant to bring blessings to my people.'

Undeterred, Taghazout devised a plan. One night, he snuck into Imalou's home and stole the carpet. Laughing, he climbed aboard and commanded it to fly him to a distant city, where he planned to sell it to the highest bidder.

As Taghazout soared through the night sky, the carpet began to shudder and weave erratically. It was no ordinary rug but one imbued with the spirit of Imalou's intentions. It resisted Taghazout's greedy commands and carried him to the middle of the Sahara, where it suddenly stopped and dropped him onto a vast, empty dune.

Panicked, Taghazout begged the carpet to return him home, but it remained motionless. Realizing his mistake, he wept and pleaded for forgiveness. The carpet finally rose, carrying him back to Imalou's village, where he fell to his knees and confessed his crime.

Imalou forgave Taghazout but warned him, 'This carpet flies not for greed or selfish desires. It serves only those with pure hearts and noble intentions.'

From then on, Imalou used the carpet to help her village thrive. She travelled to distant lands to bring back seeds for crops, knowledge of irrigation, and tales that inspired her people. The carpet became a symbol of hope, reminding everyone that great gifts must be used for the benefit of all.

When Imalou grew old, she passed the carpet down to her daughter, along with the wisdom: 'The power to rise above the earth is a gift, but the greatest power is using it to lift others.'

The Tale of the
Sword of Tamellalt

Long ago, in the fertile valley of Oukaimden, there lived a wise blacksmith named Tamellalt, whose skill with metal was unmatched.

Tamellalt was known not only for forging the sharpest swords but also for her deep understanding of the spirits of fire, metal, and water. She believed that every blade carried a purpose and a soul.

One day, a wealthy and powerful chieftain named Aghilas came to her forge. 'Tamellalt,' he said, 'I need a sword that will make me invincible. I want to conquer every tribe and rule the entire land. Can you make me such a blade?'

Tamellalt studied Aghilas with her piercing eyes. 'A sword that takes life must be balanced with one that restores it,' she said. 'Otherwise, the land will fall into ruin.'

But Aghilas laughed. 'A sword that restores life? That is nonsense! A warrior needs power, not mercy. Make me the blade I desire, and I will reward you greatly.'

Tamellalt nodded but made him no promises. She worked tirelessly for seven days and seven nights, praying to the spirits of the forge. When she emerged, she held a sword unlike any other. Its blade shimmered with an otherworldly light, and strange, intricate patterns ran along its length.

'This is the Amanar, the Life-Giver,' she told Aghilas as she handed him the sword. 'It has the power to heal wounds, mend broken bones, and even bring life back to the dying. Use it wisely.'

Aghilas scoffed but accepted the blade, thinking only of its beauty. 'A sword is a sword,' he said. 'It will serve me well.'

Soon after, he left for war, confident in his new weapon.

To his delight and amazement, the sword seemed to guide his hand, striking down his enemies with ease.

Yet, when the battles were over, he noticed something stranger than strange: the warriors he had struck down began to stir, their wounds closing as if by magic. They rose to their feet, not as enemies, but as allies, swearing loyalty to Aghilas out of gratitude for sparing their lives.

At first, Aghilas was pleased. His army grew larger with each battle, and he began to think himself unstoppable. But over time, the chieftain grew frustrated. 'What use is a sword that cannot truly conquer?' he muttered. He returned to Tamellalt's forge, demanding an explanation.

'This sword was not made for destruction,' Tamellalt said calmly. 'It restores balance, turning hatred into gratitude and enemies into friends. If you cannot see its value, then the fault lies in your heart, not the blade.'

One day, Aghilas faced a rival tribe led by a cunning warrior named Yuba. Their armies clashed in a fierce battle, but no matter how many times Aghilas wielded the Amanar, Yuba's men kept rising, joining Aghilas's forces instead of falling. Yuba, realizing the sword's secret, devised a plan. He feigned surrender and invited Aghilas to a peace talk.

During the meeting, Yuba asked, 'Why do you seek to conquer all tribes, Aghilas? Do you not see that this sword brings peace, not domination?'

Aghilas, frustrated and weary, finally saw the truth. His desire for power had only created endless cycles of conflict, while the sword's true purpose was to heal and unite.

Humbled, Aghilas laid down the Amanar and said, 'You are right. This sword is meant to restore what has been broken. I was blind to its gift.'

From that day forward, Aghilas abandoned his quest for conquest and travelled the land, using the Amanar to heal the sick, mend broken families, and bring peace to warring tribes. Over time, he became known not as a warrior, but as a peacemaker. Villages once ravaged by war began to flourish, and the land grew fertile again under his leadership.

Before his death, Aghilas returned the Amanar to Tamellalt, who hid it deep within the mountains, saying, 'This blade will remain until the land needs it again – a reminder that true strength lies not in taking life, but in restoring it.'

The Dog & the Cat

Once upon a time, not so long ago, there lived a dog named Azru and a cat named Tassila.

Azru was strong and loyal, guarding the village from wolves and thieves, while Tassila was clever and nimble, keeping homes free from mice.

Though they lived in the same village, they were rivals, each believing their work was more valuable than the other's.

One cold winter's evening, the village elder, a wise old woman named Tammuzgha, called a meeting. She spoke of a difficult journey she needed to undertake to a distant valley. She had to deliver a precious basket of seeds – seeds that could bring life to the barren fields – but the road was treacherous and long.

'I need one of you to deliver this basket safely,' Tammuzgha said. 'Who will take on this task?'

Azru stepped forward immediately. 'I am strong and fearless. I will protect the seeds from any danger.'

Tassila, not to be outdone, raised her head. 'And I am quick and cunning. I will find the safest paths.'

Tammuzgha smiled and said, 'Then you shall both go together, for strength without wisdom is dangerous, and wisdom without strength is weak.'

Reluctantly, Azru and Tassila agreed. The next morning, they set off, each determined to prove their superiority.

The first day was uneventful. Azru carried the basket with ease, his powerful legs plowing through the snow. Tassila scouted ahead, finding paths around steep cliffs and warning of hidden dangers.

But on the second day, they faced a narrow bridge over a rushing river. Azru, carrying the heavy basket, hesitated. The icy planks groaned under his weight. Tassila, light and agile, darted across to the other side.

'Come on, slowpoke!' she called out. 'Aren't you supposed to be strong?'

Azru growled. 'I won't risk the basket falling. We need a better way.'

After some thought, Azru placed the basket on a sturdy branch that had fallen nearby. He pushed the branch across the river, and Tassila used her nimble paws to guide it to safety. Working together, they crossed without losing the precious seeds.

On the third day, a snowstorm forced them to seek shelter in a dark cave. Unbeknownst to them, the cave was home to an old jackal, whose eyes gleamed with greed when he saw the basket of seeds.

'Welcome, travellers,' the jackal hissed. 'You may rest here, but the basket stays with me.'

Baring his teeth, Azru growled, 'You'll have to fight me for it.'

The jackal snarled, and the two circled each other. Tassila, observing quietly, had an idea. She crept behind the jackal and began to scratch the walls of the cave, making a sound like falling rocks.

'The cave is collapsing!' Tassila cried. 'Run for your life!'

The jackal, frightened by the echoing noise, fled into the storm. Tassila's quick thinking had saved them both.

Finally, after many days, they reached the distant valley and delivered the seeds. Tammuzgha was overjoyed. She praised both Azru's strength and Tassila's cleverness, but before they could start arguing again, she said, 'Tell me, could either of you have succeeded alone?'

Azru and Tassila looked at one another, understanding dawning in their eyes. They had faced dangers only by relying on each other's strengths.

From that day on, they no longer quarrelled but worked together for the good of the village. Azru remained the loyal protector, and Tassila the clever guide.

The villagers, inspired by their cooperation, began to value the strengths of each individual, knowing that unity was the greatest strength of all.

The Tale of the
Moon's Lesson

When the sky was a little smaller than it is today, and the birds all the bigger, there was a village in the wilds of our realm.

And, in the village, there was a young shepherd named Amrani, who was known for his restlessness and his impatience.

He longed to grow wealthy and powerful as quickly as possible, believing that the slow ways of his ancestors were deplorable beyond words.

One evening, Amrani sat on a hillside with his flock, gazing at the full moon as it bathed the land in silver light. 'Why should I toil endlessly when I can learn from the moon?' he muttered. 'It rises high and bright without effort, admired by all.'

Hearing this, the moon, wise and patient, descended from the sky in the form of an old woman draped in shimmering silver robes. 'You think my light comes without struggle, young shepherd?' she asked, her voice calm yet resonant.

Amrani, startled but emboldened, replied, 'You shine effortlessly while I labour each day. Teach me your secret, so I may rise above others.'

The moon smiled gently. 'Come, and I shall show you.' She led him on a journey through the dark valleys and peaks of the mountains.

First, they came to a deep well. The moon pointed to its dark waters. 'I do not shine by my own power,' she explained. 'I reflect the light of the sun, a constant and humble reminder that we all depend on others.'

Amrani frowned but said nothing. They continued until they reached a barren field. The moon knelt and touched the dry earth, and from her touch sprang a single, glowing flower. 'I grow brighter each night,' she said, 'but only because I fade to darkness and renew myself. Growth requires cycles of rest and humility.'

'But that takes too long!' Amrani protested. 'I want results now!'

The moon's face grew serious. 'Impatience is like this barren land, young shepherd. Without patience and care, no seeds can grow, no light can truly shine.'

Frustrated, Amrani turned to leave, but the moon raised her hand. 'Wait,' she said, her voice like the wind over the mountains. 'A final lesson.'

She led him to a vast lake where her reflection shimmered on the water. 'Look,' she said. 'When the waters are still, my reflection is clear. But when you stir them...' – she swirled her hand in the water, breaking the reflection into chaotic ripples – 'you lose sight of what is true. So it is with life. Only with patience and stillness can you see your path clearly.'

Amrani stood silently, watching the ripples settle. The moon rose back into the sky, leaving him alone with his thoughts.

From that night on, Amrani changed. He worked diligently but with patience, and his restless spirit found peace. Over time, he became a respected elder in the village, known not for his wealth or power, but for his wisdom and humility.

And when the full moon shone over the mountains, the villagers would say, 'Look! The moon smiles upon Amrani, for he has learned her lesson well.'

Finis